KITTY CORNER

OTIS

Don't miss any of these stories by Ellen Miles!

KITTY CORNER

Callie
Otis

THE PUPPY PLACE

Baxter	*Moose*
Bear	*Muttley*
Bella	*Noodle*
Buddy	*Patches*
Chewy and Chica	*Princess*
Cody	*Pugsley*
Flash	*Rascal*
Goldie	*Scout*
Honey	*Shadow*
Jack	*Snowball*
Lucky	*Sweetie*
Maggie and Max	*Ziggy*

KITTY CORNER

OTIS

ELLEN MILES

SCHOLASTIC INC.

New York   Toronto   London   Auckland
Sydney   Mexico City   New Delhi   Hong Kong

With special thanks to my
kitty expert Kristin Earhart,
for all her help.

ISBN 978-0-545-27573-6

Cover art by Mary Ann Lasher
Cover design by Tim Hall

12 11 10 9 8 7 6 5 4 3 2 1   11 12 13 14 15 16/0

Printed in the U.S.A.   40

First printing, April 2011

CHAPTER ONE

"Chicago!" Michael Battelli held up his hand for a high five.

"Chicago!" echoed his best friend, Jackson, as he smacked Michael's hand.

It was like a secret code: only they and the rest of their basketball team knew what it meant. They grinned at each other. "See you at practice tomorrow," said Michael. "I have to pick up Mia."

"See ya." Jackson waved as he headed out the door.

Bounce, bounce, bounce.

The sound echoed off the walls as Michael dribbled his basketball down the rec center's hallway. Practice had been great that day. The team had learned a new play, and Michael was still going

over the moves in his mind as he headed upstairs to meet his younger sister. He wondered what Mia had made in her art class that day.

When he arrived at Mia's art class, Michael peeked through the window in the door and spotted his sister right away. Her head was lowered and she seemed to be petting a tiny ball of clay. Mia looked toward the door and waved to Michael. He shook his head. How did she always sense the exact moment when he showed up?

Michael watched as his sister slid her art supply box onto a shelf, grabbed her backpack, and rushed over to the door. "Look!" she said. She showed him the tiny clay cat in her hand. "It's a sculpture of Callie."

Michael smiled. Mia was one cat-crazy artist! She loved to draw, paint, and sculpt cats, usually lions or tigers or other great cats that live in the wild. But after their family had fostered a stray calico kitten (they had kept her and cared for her until they found her the perfect forever home),

Mia's art had begun to feature house cats, too. Michael knew that Mia was looking forward to fostering another kitty as much as he was. Maybe even more.

"It really looks like her," Michael said. "You did a good job with the orange and black patches." Michael had always liked dogs way more than cats—until he got to know Callie. Now he loved both.

"Is it dry?" Michael asked, inspecting the paint on the clay cat. "How are you going to carry that, plus your backpack, while you're riding your scooter?"

Mia smiled up at him. "Can you carry my backpack for me?" she asked. "I don't want Callie to get smudged."

Michael sighed. Little sisters! He stuck his ball into his gym bag and grabbed Mia's backpack. "Okay, Mia, but let's take the elevator. I'm not dragging all this stuff down the stairs."

As they walked down the hall, Michael

shuffled to the left and then the right, pretending to guard another player. "Chicago!" he whispered to himself. That was the name of the play they'd learned that day. It was modeled after one that the Chicago Bulls used. Pops (that was what they all called their coach, Mr. Poplowski) had taught it to them. When Pops yelled "Chicago!" everybody worked together to get the ball to Jackson, who was the team's best shooter. It worked like a charm, and Jackson made his layup every time. Michael couldn't wait until they got to try it out in a real game against another team.

When they got to the elevator, Michael pushed the down button. While he and Mia waited for the creaky old elevator to arrive, the rec center's music teacher walked up to join them. "Hey, Battellis," Pete said. "How are you today?"

"Great," said Michael. He was taking Pete's beginning guitar class on Fridays. Pete was cool. He could play any song from the radio plus some that he wrote himself. He carried his guitar everywhere, in a zippered case slung over his shoulder.

"Your dad says this elevator is slower than dial-up Internet," Pete said with a laugh. Michael and Mia's dad was the director of the rec center, so the Battellis had known Pete for a long time. Mom had even taken them both to sing-alongs with Pete when Michael was a toddler and Mia was just a baby.

Pete pushed the elevator button again and ran his fingers through his loose brown curls. "I usually take the stairs, but today I've got this amp with me. It weighs a ton." Michael noticed the boxy black amplifier resting next to Pete's feet.

They all looked up as two girls carrying guitar cases headed toward the stairway. One, with long black hair, smiled and waved.

"Hey, Carmen," Mia said.

Michael gave a small wave, too. Carmen was in Mia's class at school. She was another cat lover, and she and Mia were becoming good friends.

Carmen also sometimes came to his guitar class. She was okay, for a third grader.

Pete hummed as he waited. "You been practicing?" he asked Michael. Michael nodded, but he didn't look Pete in the eye. Michael *had* been practicing . . . a little. But he could never sit still for long. Some nights he played for a while before he went to bed. That was about it.

"Well, I've got some great songs to teach. Get those chords down so we can have some fun," Pete said.

Michael nodded again. "I will." Practicing would be worth it if he got to play some cool songs with Pete.

At last, they heard the elevator rumble. Then the doors rattled open. Michael picked up Mia's backpack and his gym bag, and Pete grabbed his amp. Mia still held the clay Callie in her palm. As they shuffled inside, Michael noticed a crumpled fast-food bag, big enough to hold dinner for a whole family, in the back corner.

"Dad would be bummed if he saw that bag," Mia said. "He hates litter."

Mia was right. Dad was always talking about how people should treat the rec center like it was their own home. Michael wondered if the people who littered left trash all over their houses, too.

"Yeah, litter's bad news," Pete agreed. "But you know what?" He ducked his head and smiled. "It smells kind of good in here."

Michael took a deep sniff. Pete was right. Who didn't love the salty, greasy scent of fries? Michael felt his stomach rumble. He was always starving after basketball practice. Some fries would taste pretty good right about now.

"Anti-Litter Man to the rescue!" said Pete as the elevator doors clattered shut, closing them in with the smell. He put down his guitar and amp, then bent to scoop up the bag.

Hiss!

"Whoa!" Pete jumped back, tripping over his

amp. He fell with a thud to the elevator floor. "What was that?"

Michael stared at the bag. The hair on the back of his neck stood up. That sure was one strange sound coming from the empty bag!

CHAPTER TWO

Pete got to his feet and went back to the bag, shaking his head in disbelief.

Without picking it up, he unrolled the bag and tugged at the corners to open it gently. Michael held his breath.

Pete peeked inside. Then he jerked his head back and looked up at Michael and Mia.

"It's a kitten," he said. "He's tiny—and scared stiff. You two stay still while I get him out of there, okay?"

A kitten? Michael blinked at Pete. What was a kitten doing in a paper bag? In an elevator?

Michael could tell that Pete was surprised, too, even though he kept his voice calm and low. Pete gripped the top of the bag and made a steady rip down the middle. Michael and Mia both gasped when a small orange kitten appeared, cowering in the creases of a hamburger wrapper. He looked scrawny and hungry, and he trembled as he stared up at them with big, round yellow eyes.

The kitten was a tabby with orange stripes. His long white whiskers poked out from either side of his tiny pink nose and just above each eye, like eyebrows. Michael saw the kitten's fuzzy tail whip back and forth. *A dog wags his tail when he's happy,* he thought, *but that cat does not look happy at all.*

"Awww," Mia sighed. Michael quickly turned and put his finger to his lips before she could say anything else and scare the kitten. Mia's eyes opened wide and she bit her lip, so Michael knew she understood. They watched as Pete slowly reached out his hand. The kitten started to back away. He flattened his ears, squinted, and spat out another long hiss.

"It's okay, little guy." Pete's voice was so soft Michael could barely hear him. "I won't hurt you." Pete held his hand out so the kitten could smell it. Just as the kitten was about to take a step forward, the elevator thunked to a stop and its doors opened.

"Block the door!" Pete yelled. Michael jumped forward, but the orange tabby was too quick. The kitten bounded out of the elevator and took off down the first-floor hallway. Pete sighed. "I shouldn't have raised my voice," he said, shaking his head. "I scared him off."

"It's not your fault," Michael said. "We didn't block the door fast enough."

"He was so quick," Mia agreed.

"We've got to track the little guy down," Pete said. "Let's go." He grabbed his amp and guitar and leaned them against the wall. Michael did the same with his bag and Mia's, and then they all raced down the door-lined hall. Behind those closed doors, Michael knew people were doing yoga and ballet and riding exercise bikes and practicing Tai Chi. But the hall was quiet—and empty. There wasn't a kitten in sight.

"In here," Pete called. Michael and Mia followed him into a large storage room. "This door was the only one that was open. I'll bet he's hiding somewhere over there." Pete waved at a wall full of bins and shelves stuffed with everything from gymnastics mats to hand weights. Mia rushed forward, getting on her hands and knees. She crawled along, ducking her head to see under the shelves. Michael stood back and looked at all the nooks and crannies. This room was so cluttered. They could be searching for hours!

Then he heard a familiar sound.

Hiss!

"Here he is!" Mia called out. She was hunched over, looking under a cart stacked high with yoga mats.

Michael tiptoed forward and tapped his sister's back. "Mia," he whispered, "give him some space. Come talk with me and Pete. We'll figure out what to do."

Mia sighed. "At least I found him," she said as she stood up and backed away. "So how do we catch him?"

Michael wasn't sure how to catch a kitten, especially one who didn't seem very friendly. He looked around the room, trying to picture the situation as if it were a basketball play. Sometimes that was a great way to solve problems. This time, he thought of the double-teaming play that he and Jackson had learned, where two players on one team ganged up to guard one player from the other team. "Hey!" he said, pointing to a bunch of foam blocks in a crate. "Maybe we can use those." He went over and pulled a few out. "He's got himself in a corner," he said to Pete. "What if Mia and I trap him behind the cart with these? The cart is pretty high, so he probably won't try to jump it. Then maybe you can lean over and get him out."

Pete raised his eyebrows and nodded. "It could work. You'll have to be fast with the blocks, or he'll slip out."

Michael and Mia looked at each other, smiled, and nodded. "We can do it," Michael said.

"Okay, let's give it a try." Pete closed the door to the hallway.

Michael slid the crate of blocks over to where the kitten was hiding. "Ready?" he asked.

"Ready," said Mia.

As fast as they could, Mia and Michael lined up all the blocks so they filled the space under the cart, without a single opening for the kitten to escape through.

"Okay, Pete," Michael said.

Pete came up and leaned over the cart. "Hey, little fella," Pete said softly. "We're just trying to

help you." Pete stretched out his arm and made a soft *wsshhh-wsshhh* sound.

Peeking between the stacks of yoga mats, Michael could see the little kitten looking up at Pete, his yellow eyes wide with fear.

I'm scared! I don't know if you're a friend or an enemy.

"That's it. Stay right there. Okay. I gotcha," Pete murmured softly. Then he started to straighten up, his hand under the tabby's belly. The kitten's orange-striped legs hung loosely in the air.

"Nice teamwork, guys," Pete said as he pulled the kitten to his chest.

"Good plan, big brother." Mia nudged Michael in the ribs with her elbow. He grinned at her, then stood up and peered at the kitten cradled in Pete's arms. There was still a little French fry salt on his whiskers. He didn't look fierce at all. He was adorable, even though his fur was sticky and matted in places.

"Why would anybody leave a little kitten behind like that, stuck in a bag like he was garbage?" Michael asked. It made him mad. How could people treat animals so badly?

Pete shook his head. "Who knows? He must have been left here. I haven't seen any missing-kitten posters around. Anyway, at least we rescued the little guy," he said. "Now what?"

"We should make sure he's not hurt," Mia suggested.

Pete held up the tiny tabby cat, both hands just under the kitten's front legs, and looked into his big yellow eyes. "Are you okay, fella?" The kitten let out a raspy meow, and his tiny pink nose quivered. "You look pretty good for someone who's been stuffed into a paper bag. You're much cuter than a hamburger, but you should still see a vet.

And"—Pete wrinkled his own nose—"you sure could use a bath!"

The tabby blinked up at Pete.

First I was stuck in that bag. Now here I am hanging up in the air! But I feel safe. This guy's hands are strong and warm. His voice is kind and low. I think I can trust him. I hope I can.

Michael laughed. The kitten's wide-eyed expression was hilarious. It was almost as if the tabby understood what Pete was saying.

"We could take him to Dr. Bulford, at Wags and Whiskers," Mia said. She clasped her hands together and bounced on her toes. "That's where we took Callie."

"Who's Callie?" Pete asked. While Michael told Pete all about Callie, Mia scratched the tabby kitten under his chin and whispered into his little pointy ears.

"We could foster this kitten, too, right?" she asked Michael. "He needs help. He needs a family of his own."

Michael swallowed. He looked from Mia to the tiny tabby to Pete. It was true. The kitten did need a family, but were they the family he needed?

CHAPTER THREE

"I don't know, Mia," said Michael. As cute as the kitten was, Michael knew he had to be practical. "How would we get him home? We have our scooters, remember? Besides," he added, "Mom and Dad wouldn't want us to just show up with another kitten. You know they'd at least want to have a family chat first."

"He's purring," Mia cooed. "You can feel it. Right here."

Michael reached out and touched the kitten's throat. He laughed at the way the purr tickled as it vibrated through his hand. Funny how just a few minutes earlier the little cat had been acting feisty and mean, but now he seemed sweet and content. How could his mood change so fast?

"Well, I guess I could take the little dude," Pete offered. "At least for now. I might even have some time to get him to a vet."

"Oh," Mia said. Michael could tell she was disappointed. Then she brightened. "Can we come visit him?" she asked.

"Of course," Pete said. "I haven't had a cat since I was a kid, so I might need some advice."

"Absolutely." Mia grinned at Pete. "I know all about cats." She held the kitten while Pete put away his amp and got ready to leave the rec center. Michael knew the little tabby would be safe with Pete. Still, as they said good-bye at the main entrance, he couldn't resist petting the kitten one more time. Pete had zipped him inside his jacket. Just the kitten's head and front paws poked out.

"See you, little guy," Michael said. He gave the tabby a rub under his chin. He could feel the rumbling purr again, just under the kitten's fluffy fur.

"See you in class on Friday," Pete said.

"Yup, see you in class." Michael swung his gym bag over one shoulder and Mia's backpack over the other.

"Good-bye, kitten," Mia called with a wave as she and Michael grabbed their scooters and headed home.

As soon as they arrived, Mia rushed up the stairs and into their apartment building. By the time Michael parked both scooters, he could hear that she was already in the kitchen, telling Mom everything. Michael stepped into the kitchen, put a permission slip he needed for school on the counter, and opened the fridge.

"Hey, Michael, no big snacks, okay?" Mom said as she wiped off a cutting board. "Dinner will be ready soon, sweetie. Sorry I interrupted, Mia." She smiled at Mia, who launched into her story again. She talked fast until she was at the part where Pete had agreed to take the kitten home.

"Well, thank goodness for that," Mom said. "I'm

not sure we're ready to foster another kitten so soon."

"We're not fostering him," Michael said, his head still ducked inside the fridge. "Pete is. We never would have brought a cat home without asking you first." He pulled out a couple of cheese sticks and shut the door.

"I'm glad to hear it," Mom replied. She raised her eyebrows and looked Michael in the eye. He knew that look. Man, it was a good thing they hadn't brought that kitten home! Then he heard the jangle of keys that meant Dad was home from work. He'd probably left the rec center right after Mia and Michael had zoomed off on their scooters.

Michael flattened himself against the cupboard as Mia darted past. She met Dad at the apartment door and tugged him into the kitchen. "You won't believe what happened today," she was saying as she pulled him along. She began to tell the story all over again, starting with the crumpled bag in the elevator.

"Wait," Dad said, holding up both hands to get everyone's attention. "Are you telling me that Pete let the cat out of the bag?" Dad laughed to himself and looked around to see if anyone else got his joke.

"Dad, it's not funny," Mia insisted, hands on her hips. "The kitten was really scared."

Sometimes Michael thought Mia took things too seriously, but this time she was right. "It's true, Dad. The kitten was freaked out. He hated being in that bag."

"Okay, I'm sorry," Dad said. "Mia, go ahead with your story." He squeezed Michael's shoulder and walked over to give Mom a kiss.

As Mia told the story a second time, Michael thought again about how mean the kitten had seemed at first. What was all that hissing about? There was a lot he didn't know about cats. He decided he would use his computer time that night to do some research. Maybe he could figure out why the kitten had hissed, and why he had begun to purr the instant Pete had picked him up.

After dinner, Michael had just turned on the computer when he heard the phone ring. It was Mom's night to work late, and Dad was reading a bedtime story with Mia, so Michael answered. "Hello?"

"Hey, Michael, it's Pete."

Michael gulped. He should be practicing his guitar instead of spending time online. But Pete probably hadn't called to nag him about that. "Hi," he said. "How's the kitten?"

Pete didn't answer right away. "Is your dad there?" he asked.

"Um, yeah," Michael said. "But he's putting Mia to bed. Can I have him call you back?"

Pete sighed. "Sure. It's about Otis. The kitten, I mean. I named him Otis."

"Otis?" Michael liked the name. It sounded just right for the little orange tabby. "Why Otis?"

"It's a brand of elevator," Pete said. "Maybe you never noticed, but there's a little nameplate that says 'Otis' on most elevators. Plus, there was a singer named Otis Redding, who sang some of my all-time favorite songs." Pete sighed again. "Anyway, I was hoping your family could foster him after all."

Michael wasn't sure what to say. He had liked that little kitten right away, and he would love to have Otis come to stay for a while. But would his parents agree? Mom had already said she probably wasn't ready to foster another cat.

"Listen, Michael," Pete said. "I know it's a lot to ask. Otis is fine. He's a really cool little guy. I'm just not sure he's a good fit for me. He doesn't seem too comfortable here. Talk to your folks, and call me back. I could bring him over tonight."

"Okay." Michael said good-bye and hung up, wondering how in the world he could convince his parents to take on another foster kitten.

CHAPTER FOUR

Michael heard Mia's bedroom door close. That meant Dad had finished reading to her. Michael took a deep breath. He had to convince Dad that they should foster Otis. But how?

Dad appeared in the doorway. "Hey, how was practice today?" he asked.

Michael frowned. Basketball was the last thing on his mind right now. "Okay, I guess," he said. "Can I talk to you about something else?"

"Of course." Dad reached out to squeeze Michael's shoulder. "What is it?"

Michael decided just to tell Dad everything. "Pete called. He wants us to foster Otis."

Dad raised his eyebrows, as if to say, *Go on.*

"Otis is what he named the kitten, after

Otis elevators," Michael continued. "And some singer."

"Ah, yes. Otis Redding, the King of Soul," Dad said.

Michael took another deep breath. "Pete said he wasn't sure that keeping Otis was going to work out, and he wants to bring him over here . . . tonight."

Dad looked surprised. "Tonight?"

"Pete sounded really upset," Michael added. "And Otis has nowhere else to go."

"You know it isn't just up to me." Dad gave Michael a serious look. "We have to check with Mom."

"Yeah, but what's the chance we'll convince her?" Michael kicked his toe against the kitchen cabinet. Mom was probably closing up the garden shop now and wouldn't be home until after his bedtime. He knew she wasn't crazy about the idea of taking in another kitten. What would Pete do with Otis if she said no?

"Why don't you give her a call?" Dad suggested. "Just tell her what you told me. You can write down the major points before you call, so you don't forget. Then she and I can discuss it while you get ready for bed."

Michael sat down with a pencil and paper. A few minutes later, he called Mom. He was so nervous he raced through his list of Reasons We Should Foster Otis. He paused before the last one. "It would be a huge help to Pete," Michael finished. He waited hopefully for Mom's reaction. Had he been convincing? Had he talked Mom into it? Mia probably would have been better at this.

"Well, I don't know, honey," Mom said after a little while. "A kitten that young might be a lot of work."

Michael grinned into the phone. This was promising. "I don't know" was a whole lot better than "no." He pressed on. "You know Mia and I will help."

Mom was quiet on the other end. "Pete has done plenty for us over the years," she finally said. "I guess we owe him a favor. Let me talk to your father for a moment."

Michael handed Dad the phone and watched his expression as he talked things over with Mom. He was smiling. That was good news, right? Dad passed the phone back to Michael and said, "Your mother wants to talk to you again."

Michael held his breath until Mom began to speak.

"All right, tell Pete we'll take Otis," she said. "But remember, we are only fostering. And I don't want you staying up late waiting for this kitten. If Pete doesn't come in half an hour, you have to go to bed, mister."

Yes! Michael clenched his fist as if he'd just made a great basketball play. Then he froze, a little surprised at himself. Why was he so happy about a silly cat? Mia would be thrilled, but then she was a cat lover to begin with.

"Thanks, Mom," Michael said. "You're going to love Otis."

"I'm sure I will," Mom said. Michael could tell by her voice that she was smiling.

Michael said good-bye, then headed straight for the hall closet. He knew that Mom had stored all the cat stuff there after they had found a home for Callie.

While Dad called Pete, Michael pulled out the litter box, a blanket for a bed, kitten food, and a few toys. Michael wanted to have everything set up before Pete came.

While Michael got things ready for Otis, he kept his eye on the clock, hoping Pete and the kitten would get there before he had to go to bed. He was in his room when he heard the buzzer. Michael raced out of the apartment and into the hallway, still pulling on his pajama top. He could see Pete through the glass in the building's big front door.

"Hi, Pete," Michael said as he unbolted the door and pulled it open.

"Hey, Michael. Thanks for helping me out," Pete said as he came into the hallway. He had a backpack on backward, so the bag part was on his chest. "You want to say hi, Otis?" Pete asked in a soft voice. Pete leaned over, and Michael could see that the little tabby was inside the backpack. Only his fluffy head stuck out. He yawned, showing his pink tongue and tiny needle-sharp teeth.

Oh, no. Another new place? I was just getting used to the old one. All I need is a quiet spot to go to sleep. I hope I can take a nice nap here.

"Hi, Otis," Michael said as he scratched the kitten behind the ears. "Do you remember me? You're going to stay here for a while."

"How long are you guys going to stand

out there in the hall?" Dad called from the apartment door.

"Coming, Joe," Pete said as he followed Michael down the hallway. Once they were inside the Battellis' apartment, Michael and Pete sat down on the couch and Dad sank into his favorite seat, the old rocking chair. Pete smiled as he unzipped his backpack. "There you go, buddy. I know you want out."

Otis looked around, then slowly stepped out of the bag. He tested his footing on the shaggy rug and sniffed in all directions. His whiskers quivered and his ears twitched. Michael thought Otis looked nervous. That was a bummer. He had hoped the kitten would feel at home right away.

"He's a great kitten," Pete said. He picked up Otis with one hand, and the kitten promptly snuggled into his lap. "He used the litter box and he was really good at the vet. We played a little this afternoon and he fell asleep while I was practicing guitar." Michael noticed that Pete's smile began to fade as he continued. "But then he got really scared when my band came for rehearsal this evening. As soon as he heard the drums, he raced into my room and hid under the bed. He hissed whenever anyone tried to get him out." Pete shook his head. "I just can't have a cat who doesn't like music, or other people. There's always a lot going on at my place. I don't think he'd be happy with me. And the vet said it was important for Otis to get settled in a forever home as soon as possible."

Michael looked at Otis, curled up in Pete's lap. The kitten had closed his eyes and tucked his nose under his tail. "He sure seems to like you now," Michael blurted out. "I mean, Otis looks really happy."

"Well, he wasn't before." Pete scratched one of the kitten's orange ears. "He hated my band's music. I think he needs a quieter home. That's why I brought him here."

Michael looked down at his feet and nodded. Pete was a good guy, and Michael really liked him. But he couldn't help thinking that Pete was making a big mistake. How could he give up a kitten as sweet as Otis?

CHAPTER FIVE

Michael woke from a deep sleep to a loud, piercing sound. As he sat up in bed, rubbing his eyes, he realized that the sound had to be Otis, yowling his head off. How could such a little kitten make so much noise? Was he sick? Michael stumbled through the dark apartment into the family room and found Mom next to Otis's bed. She was petting him and speaking softly, trying to calm him down. "Go back to sleep, Michael," she whispered. "He'll be fine."

Michael was so tired he didn't argue. He headed straight to his room and climbed back into bed. As he fell asleep, he thought he might have been wrong about Otis and Pete's being perfect for each other. How could Pete—or anyone—deal with a cat who yowled all night long? It wasn't going to be easy to find a home for the noisy kitten.

The next morning, he realized he'd been right about one thing: Mia was thrilled when she woke up and discovered that Otis was there. The second she spotted the kitten on his little blanket-bed on the couch, she squealed and ran straight toward him. Otis leapt to his feet, then froze. His hair stood up and he arched his back. When Mia reached for him, he jumped off the couch and scurried across the floor to hide under the side table.

Mia knelt down and looked under the table. "Here, kitty."

"Mia, sweetie," Mom said, "you need to give him a little time. He's still getting used to us. Let's let him hide down there for a while. He needs to have a quiet, safe place to go when he feels scared."

"Otis doesn't like loud noises," Michael said as

he swirled a spoon through his cereal. Mia looked at him doubtfully. "Pete said so. We have to be careful."

"I'll be careful," Mia said. She sat down at the table and began to eat her oatmeal.

"Pete also said he needs a bath."

"Oh, can I help?" Mia asked immediately. "And can Carmen come over to help, too?"

"I don't know," Michael began. "That might be too much for Otis."

"I think it's fine," Dad answered as he sat down with his coffee. "You could probably use the extra hands. Most cats don't like water."

"Great." Mia smiled happily. "I'll ask her at school."

Michael frowned at Dad. Then he looked at Otis. The kitten was still under the table, but now he was busy playing. He rolled around on his back, his paws stretched wide as he grabbed at a tassel on the rug and nibbled it. He looked happy. Maybe Dad was right. Maybe it wasn't such a big deal if both Mia and Carmen helped with his bath.

Later that day, as they walked home from school, Michael reminded Mia and Carmen about how timid and shy Otis could be. "And remember what Dad said," he told Mia. "We'll have to take it slow with this bath thing. Cats don't like water."

"Most cats," Mia corrected him. "But jaguars love water. They swim and play in the water all the time. Maybe Otis is like a jaguar."

"Yeah, maybe," Carmen agreed.

Michael shook his head as he opened the door to their brownstone building. Mia was always full of facts about the great cats. "Find Otis," he told her. "Try to pet him and keep him calm. He needs to be relaxed." As the girls ran into the apartment, Michael added, "I'll get stuff ready for the bath."

During computer time at school, Jackson and Michael had looked up how to give a cat a bath.

Now he looked over the list they'd made one more time. It didn't sound too hard, as long as you planned on getting wet. Still, Michael had no idea how Otis would react.

Mom had set aside a few old towels. Michael rounded up some baby shampoo, a little comb, and a plastic cup for pouring small amounts of water on Otis. *Check, check, check.* That was everything on the list. They were just about all set. Michael started the bathwater and held his hand under it to make sure it wasn't too warm. They didn't need much water. Otis was so small! He turned off the faucet and headed for the family room.

"Hey, where are you?" he called. He hoped Otis hadn't managed to run away like Callie had. That calico cat had been a real escape artist.

"In here, Michael." Michael followed Mom's voice to Mia's room. When he looked in, he saw Otis sleeping in Mia's lap. Carmen was petting the creamy fur under his chin.

"The girls are trying to soothe Otis before his bath," Mom said.

"Good," replied Michael. "We need to keep him calm and work fast." Otis barely opened his eyes when Michael lifted him and carried him to the bathroom.

Michael gently lowered Otis into the tub as Mia and Carmen crowded around. Otis's eyes popped open the instant his paws hit the water, and he crouched down with a low yowl, ready to leap out.

What's happening? Why am I wet? I don't like it.

"Mia, can you keep him in there without hurting him?" Michael asked.

"Of course," Mia said. She reached forward to hold him just behind his front legs. Otis let out a tiny mew.

"It's okay, boy. We'll make this nice and quick. I just need to get you wet so I can wash some of this crusty stuff off you." Jackson and Michael had read that cats rarely need baths, since they clean themselves, but Otis was really dirty. The fur on his belly was sticky and matted. Michael guessed it might be dried ketchup from the fast-food bag. He took the plastic cup and poured water over Otis's back. Would the kitten try to jump out? Or would he yowl again, the way he had in the middle of the night?

"What a good cat!" Carmen exclaimed. "He didn't even flinch." She reached forward and scratched him between the ears.

Michael had to agree. He could hardly believe it. Otis stood quietly while Michael lathered his fur with the shampoo. He seemed to like Carmen's petting. He even tilted his head so she could get behind his ear.

"He's so tiny when he's wet," Mia said.

"And I thought he looked scrawny before," Carmen said.

"He's just a small fry. He'll get bigger," Michael told her.

Mia laughed. "Very funny, Michael."

"Huh?" Michael wasn't sure what she meant. He was focused on rinsing Otis.

"Remember when we found him in the elevator?" Mia asked. "It smelled like fries. And you just called him small fry. Get it?"

Michael rolled his eyes.

"Small fry!" Carmen let out a hearty laugh. She leaned her head into the tub, putting her nose right up to Otis's face. "Are you a small fry, Otis?" she asked in a baby voice.

Otis opened his eyes wide and let out a hiss.

Too close! Too close! Get away!

The kitten's ears went back and he whipped out his paw. Carmen did not even have a chance to get out of the way.

CHAPTER SIX

"Ow! He scratched me!" Carmen jumped back and touched her finger to her nose.

Michael felt his stomach jump when he saw the angry red line where blood was welling up. "You were in his face. What did you expect?" Michael glared at Carmen, then turned to Otis. The kitten was sopping wet and covered with suds. His ears drooped.

"Mom!" Mia yelled. "Otis scratched Carmen!"

Michael gulped. Why had he yelled at Carmen like that? It wasn't really her fault. His heart raced as he quickly poured several cups of water over Otis's back. Then he pulled the kitten from Mia's grasp and wrapped him in a towel.

Michael heard Mom's hurried footsteps. He

held Otis tightly to his chest and softly scratched the damp fur behind his ears. "It's okay, Otis," he whispered. "She didn't mean to scare you."

Otis shivered, and blinked up at Michael.

Thank goodness I'm out of the water. Now I'm cold, but it's warm in the boy's arms.

Michael's chest felt tight when he looked down at the little kitten. He wanted to protect Otis and keep him safe. In fact, maybe he wanted to keep him forever! If Pete really didn't want this sweet little tabby, maybe Otis should stay right where he was, with the Battellis.

Mom appeared, looking worried. "Oh, Carmen, sweetie," she said, when she saw the red streak across Carmen's nose. Mom rested one hand on Carmen's head and opened the medicine cabinet with the other.

"What happened?" she asked. She looked right at Michael.

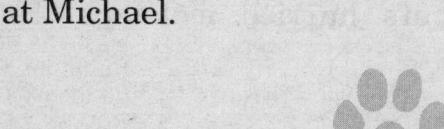

He swallowed. "She got too close. She was right up in his face."

"It wasn't Carmen's fault," Mia said, hands on her hips.

"No, it wasn't," Michael admitted. "Otis doesn't trust her." He took a deep breath. "He doesn't trust anyone." He glanced at Carmen. "Sorry I yelled."

"It's okay," Carmen whispered, but her eyes were brimming with tears.

Michael looked away.

"Michael, you and I need to have a talk." Mom sighed. She wetted a cotton ball with liquid from a brown bottle.

Michael frowned. *A talk?* he thought. *Great.* Would Mom send Otis away? There was no way she'd put up with a cat who scratched people.

"Carmen, this will only sting for a second," Mom promised. "I just need to clean it out." The liquid made bubbles in the red line across Carmen's nose when Mom pulled the cotton away.

"Ow! I mean, I'm okay." Carmen smiled up at

Mom. "I didn't mean to scare him. He just looked so cute."

"I told you guys you had to be careful," Michael said.

Mia spun around to face Michael. "Why are you being such a know-it-all? Carmen and I have read tons about cats. You don't know anything."

Michael took another deep breath. "I've been doing some reading, too. Otis was abandoned. He was left all alone. I read that abandoned cats can be more nervous and scared than other cats. That's why I yelled at you, Carmen. I was just worried about Otis. I'm really sorry." How many times was he going to have to apologize?

"It's okay," Carmen said again.

Michael felt the kitten squirm, so he put Otis on the floor. Otis gave a tiny mew, looked around, then shook his entire body. Drops of water flew everywhere.

Michael tried not to laugh. But when he looked around, he noticed that everyone else was cracking up. Even Mom was smiling. "Is he rinsed off?" she asked.

"Pretty much," Michael said.

"Then you need to come with me. Otis can stay here with the girls." Michael didn't want to leave Otis, but at least he was sure that Carmen and Mia would be more careful with the kitten now.

Michael followed Mom into the kitchen. She turned back to face him. "Honey, you know you can't talk to Carmen that way. She's our guest, and she's trying to help."

"I know. It just came out," Michael said. "I was so worried about Otis."

"I'm worried, too," Mom admitted. "He's sweet, but he isn't really settling in."

"That's exactly what Pete said," Michael mumbled.

"What else did Pete say?" Mom tilted her head to one side and looked into Michael's eyes.

"He said that the vet thinks Otis needs to find his forever family soon." Michael crossed his

fingers and hoped Mom might decide that Otis should just stay with them. If Pete didn't want him, Michael sure did. Even with all the yowling, Otis was one terrific kitten.

"You should call Dr. Bulford and find out why she said that. It might help us help Otis."

"Can you call her?" Michael kicked his toe against the floor. He felt a little shy about calling the vet, even though he'd talked to her lots of times in person.

"Remember how you said you and Mia would help with Otis?" Mom asked. "I think this would be a good job for you." Mom gave him an encouraging smile. "I'll go see how the girls are doing."

"Okay." Michael trudged over to the laptop to look up the vet's number.

He was relieved when he heard Dr. Bulford's voice. She was always so nice. Michael quickly told her about how Otis had scratched Carmen's nose. "That sounds like a normal response," Dr. Bulford said. "Lots of cats are afraid of baths, and they often scratch when they're scared. It's their way of protecting themselves."

Michael let out a sigh. "Otis seems scared a lot. His yowling woke us up last night."

"It's going to take him time to feel comfortable," Dr. Bulford said. "He needs to learn to trust you. That's why I think it would be good to find him a permanent home soon. It'll be hard for him to settle in with your family and then have to move on to someone new."

After they'd talked a little more, Michael thanked Dr. Bulford and hung up. He found everyone in the family room. Carmen was dangling a piece of red string in the air, and Otis was sitting up on his hind legs. He batted the string back and forth. His eyes were bright and wide.

"What did Dr. Bulford say?" Mom asked.

"She said that Otis needs a real home to feel safe," Michael told them. "And she said he needs a routine. It'll help him adjust. Like she said we should always feed him at the same time, in the same place, and we should let him have a safe place where we don't bug him. Like his bed. Or under the table where he was hiding earlier. Stuff like that."

"We can do that," Mia said.

Mom nodded. "Good. But don't forget we also need to try to find Otis a home. Maybe"—she thought for a moment—"maybe the two of you could make some flyers to put up around the neighborhood. With luck, we'll find him a forever family soon."

"Great idea," said Mia.

Michael looked at her. Didn't she want to keep Otis, like he did? She gave him a little smile, and he understood. Mom needed to know that they were working hard to find Otis a home. He nodded. "Sure. We can make the flyers after school tomorrow."

Mom smiled. "Great. I know we all want what's best for Otis."

CHAPTER SEVEN

Michael was exhausted the next day. Otis had prowled around and yowled all night. At one point in the middle of the night, Michael had woken just in time to see Otis walk into his room and sniff around. Michael blinked, bleary-eyed, and wondered if the kitten might be looking for something. He got out of bed to refill his food dish and give him fresh water. He tried to pet him, but Otis wouldn't stay still. Finally, Michael went back to his room, closed the door, and turned on a fan to drown out the mournful meows.

Somehow, Mia slept right through the noise. In the morning she was bright-eyed and happy to see Otis. Michael couldn't believe it. He felt like he could hardly hold up his head.

"Don't forget we have to make the flyers this afternoon," Michael reminded Mia.

Mia stuck out her bottom lip, pouting.

"You know we have to find him a home," Michael said. He and Mia had talked it all through the day before, after Carmen had left. If they agreed to make the flyers, it would give them more time to convince Mom that they should keep Otis. But now Michael was starting to think that maybe the kitten needed a different home, a home of his own where he could yowl all night at somebody else. "Otis really needs a forever family."

"And I really need a full night's sleep," Mom said as she sat down at the table.

"I'm starting to think Pete knew something when he named him after Otis Redding," Dad said from the kitchen doorway. "That cat sure can sing the blues."

"Cats are nocturnal." Mia bit into her bagel. "In the wild, they hunt at night and sleep during the day. But I read that most house cats learn to sleep when their families do."

"Not Otis," Michael grumbled. "Last night he woke me up three times." Michael looked over at Otis, who was snoozing on his bed by the sofa.

Dad took a gulp of coffee. "If this keeps up, we're all going to be singing the blues."

After school, Mia and Michael snacked on brownies while they worked on the flyer. They used a picture of Otis playing with the red string. His yellow eyes were bright and sparkly, and he almost looked like he was smiling. Michael didn't think anyone would ever believe that the happy little kitten in the picture could make such a loud, sad meow.

"'Meet Otis.'" Michael read the poster headline out loud. "'He needs a loving home. Will you adopt him?'" Underneath that, he typed "Call the Battellis," and put in their phone number.

"It seems short," Mia said. "Shouldn't we tell more about him?"

"I think this is good for now. I bet we get lots of calls," said Michael. "Then we can pick the best family." If the Battellis weren't keeping him, Michael wasn't going to let Otis go to just any home. He wanted to ask lots of questions. He wanted to make sure that Otis's new owner was the perfect match for him.

They printed out twenty flyers on plain white typing paper. "We can hang them on light posts," Mia said.

"And in shopwindows," Michael added. Mr. Li's grocery, Mrs. Lopez's bakery, the drugstore, and the bagel shop on the corner—they all had bulletin boards where people advertised things like concerts or classes or yard sales. Why not a cute little kitten?

Before they left the apartment, Michael and Mia stopped by the windowsill where Otis was snoozing. He barely lifted his head as they gave him a quick scratch under the chin. He squinted his eyes contentedly.

Mmm, that feels nice. I feel safe here. I can keep sleeping.

They walked around the neighborhood carrying the flyers and a roll of tape. Mia held each flyer in place, and Michael taped it up. As they passed people on the sidewalk, Michael wondered if any of them would want to adopt Otis. The more people he saw, the more he worried. How would he know what questions to ask when people came to look at Otis? How would he know for sure that Otis was going to a good home?

That night, Michael lay in bed, reading. Even though he had music playing on his iPod, he could hear Otis starting up his evening yowl. It was funny how the kitten's pitiful meows seemed to rise and fall in time with the music. The meows grew louder, and soon Michael looked up to see Otis pushing his head through the partly opened door.

Otis stuck his pink nose in the air and sniffed around. He tilted his head to one side. He flicked his fluffy orange ear and padded over to Michael's iPod and speakers. He batted the iPod with his paw. He looked right at Michael and yowled.

"What is it, Otis?" Michael asked. "What's going on, boy?"

Otis stood there for a moment. Then he took a few steps over to a dirty basketball jersey that Michael had thrown on the floor. Otis sniffed the shirt, then started to knead it with his paws. He purred.

This seems like a good place to sleep. Not too quiet, not too loud. It's cozy, and it's close to the boy. I'll just lie down for a little while.

"You purr almost as loud as you yowl," Michael said. Otis's purring sounded like it was part of the song. It had the same easy rhythm. Michael laughed. Otis didn't notice. He curled up on the shirt and closed his eyes.

Michael turned off the light and closed his own eyes.

When Michael woke up in the morning, he felt better. He had actually slept! He remembered Otis yowling around five or six o'clock. But Michael had fallen back to sleep—had Otis slept in his room that whole time? *Maybe it was the music,* Michael thought. He remembered Pete saying that Otis had napped while he practiced the guitar. Soft music and a sleepy, quiet cat. Michael thought there might be a connection. But how could he find out for sure? It was time to make a plan.

CHAPTER EIGHT

Michael had been so busy thinking about his plan, he'd almost forgotten about the flyers he and Mia had put up. But when the phone rang during breakfast that morning, his heart began to race. Maybe it was someone calling about Otis.

Michael was too nervous to listen to Mom's end of the phone call. What if someone adopted Otis that day? Then he'd never get to test his plan.

"That was not the call I expected," Mom said when she hung up the phone.

"Someone saw the flyer?" Mia asked. Michael could tell she was already disappointed.

"Yes," Mom said. "Pete. He wants to see Otis again before he goes to a new home."

Michael's heart jumped.

"That's nice," Dad said as he closed the laptop on the kitchen counter. "I know he felt bad that Otis wasn't a good match for him."

"But—" Michael stopped himself. He was pretty sure Otis and Pete were a perfect match, after all. But he wasn't quite ready to tell his parents about his plan. He got up from the table and went to his room. Mia followed him.

"You have an idea, don't you?" Mia asked. "I can tell by the look in your eyes." She poked him. "Come on, tell me."

"It's probably nothing," Michael said. He shoved a book into his backpack. "Otis fell asleep in here last night. I had some soft music on, and he came in and started purring. Then he conked out."

"I thought Otis didn't like music," Mia said.

"That's what Pete said. But what if he's wrong? Maybe Otis was just scared because Pete's band practice was so loud. Maybe it's fine if it's just Pete and his guitar." Michael looked at his sister. She did not seem convinced.

"Maybe Pete just doesn't want a kitten," Mia said.

"I don't think that's it." Michael shook his head. "Pete didn't give Otis enough of a chance. I think they're meant for each other—if I'm right about Otis liking music. I'm going to test my theory out tonight." Michael motioned his head toward his iPod speakers. "First I have to be sure that soft music really does calm Otis down. Then maybe I can get Pete to change his mind about keeping him."

The doorbell rang.

"I hope it works," Mia said. She shrugged and walked out.

Michael put the rest of his school stuff in his backpack. When he got to the family room, he saw that Pete was sitting on the couch. Otis laced himself around Pete's legs with a rumbly purr.

This guy came back. The guy with the low voice.

I'm glad he's here. He's good at petting. I want him to pet me right now.

Otis took a big leap and landed lightly in Pete's lap. "Hi, there, Otis," Pete said with a laugh as the kitten curled up cozily. "You're looking good, little dude."

"He really likes you, Pete," Mom said. "He doesn't jump up on us like that."

"I really like him, too," Pete said. He absent-mindedly scratched Otis's belly, and the kitten rubbed his mouth up against Pete's hand. "But I just can't have a cat who doesn't like music. There's no way it would work out."

Michael wondered if he should say something to Pete right then. Otis looked so happy. It was obvious they were good together. But wouldn't it be better if he waited until he was sure that Otis liked soft music?

Mia nudged Michael and rushed out of the

room. She came back with the family camera and snapped a shot of Otis and Pete.

At the click, Pete seemed to remember something. "Well, I gotta run. I just wanted to see Otis again," he said as he gently scooted Otis onto the couch. "Thanks for letting me barge in, Battellis."

"Anytime, Pete," Dad said.

Pete gave Michael a slap on the shoulder. "See you in class, bud."

After Pete left, the Battellis went back to their morning routines. Michael and Mia grabbed their lunches, petted Otis, and left for school with Dad.

"Is there anything you want to talk about?" Dad asked as they crunched through the leaves on the sidewalk.

Michael looked up at his father. How did he always know when Michael had something on his mind?

"Michael thinks Pete should adopt Otis," Mia said.

Michael rolled his eyes.

"I think that's a great idea," Dad said. "But Pete doesn't seem so sure. It wouldn't be right for us to force someone to take a kitten. Pete has to really want Otis or it isn't a good match for either of them." The three of them stopped at the school steps. "Don't worry. We'll find Otis a good home." Dad gave them each a hug, and Michael and Mia headed into school.

Michael thought about Otis all day, between classes and during lunch.

"What's going on?" Jackson asked as they sat down at their usual table in the cafeteria. "I didn't see you before school."

Michael unwrapped his sandwich and stared at it. Tuna on rye. Not his favorite. "I was late. Pete came by to see Otis again." He had already told Jackson all about Otis and how he thought Pete and the cat were perfect for each other.

"Great! So he's taking him?" Jackson pulled two oatmeal-raisin cookies out of his bag and handed one to Michael.

Michael bit into the cookie and shook his head. "Not so far," he said. "But I'm still working on it."

That night, Michael checked to see if Otis was still sleeping on his bed of blankets by the couch. The kitten was curled up, his chin resting on his front paws. He sure was cute when he was sleeping! Michael went to his room and set up his iPod. He programmed the playlist to repeat all night. Next he checked his calendar. He had guitar class the next day. If all went according to plan, he'd have good news for Pete.

When the door opened, Michael thought it was Otis, pushing his way into Michael's room. But it was Dad. "Hey, buddy," he said. "Ready for bed?"

"Almost," Michael said. He moved the dirty jersey Otis had slept on the night before, putting it closer to the speakers.

"Shouldn't that shirt be in the laundry hamper?" Dad asked.

Michael glanced up at Dad. "Otis is practicing a new trick," he said.

Dad raised his eyebrows.

"He's going to lie down here and sleep through the night." Michael gave the shirt a pat.

"Oh, yeah?" Dad asked. "No yowling at the moon?"

"No yowling at the moon."

"I'll believe it when I don't hear it," Dad said.

He walked over to give Michael a good-night kiss.

"Leave the door open a little," Michael said.

As Dad turned off the light, Michael nestled under his favorite NBA blanket and waited. It wasn't long before he heard a familiar yowl. A minute later he heard another yowl, closer now. He opened his eyes to see Otis kneading the shirt with his paws, then settling in, curled up nose to tail.

Oh, good. It's just right in here. I like this music. And this shirt is really comfy. Now I can get some rest. I think I'll stay right here next to the boy all night.

"Night, Otis." Michael could hear the kitten's rumbly purr. "Sleep well—please, please sleep well!"

CHAPTER NINE

Michael woke to the smell of pancakes. He jumped out of bed and rushed to the family room. Mom and Mia were already sitting at the table.

"Morning, sleepyhead," Mom said.

"Pancakes!" Mia declared. She pointed at her plate. "On a school day!"

"Is it a special occasion?" Michael asked.

Mom smiled. "I was so tired last night that I must have slept right through Otis's yowling. I guess we're celebrating a full night's sleep."

"You didn't sleep through his yowling," Michael said as he sat down. "He didn't yowl at all." Michael glanced at Otis, who was snoozing on his bed of blankets.

"Are you sure?"

Michael's mouth was full of fluffy pancake, so he just nodded.

"How do you know?" Mom squinted when she asked, like a detective grilling a suspect.

Michael quickly swallowed and told her all about his theory and how he had tested it. "It worked! With the soft music on, Otis slept and didn't yowl. Two nights in a row."

Mom nodded. "Maybe it's the music, or maybe Otis just doesn't like for it to be too quiet," she said. "He always takes his morning catnap in the family room, and it's never quiet in here."

"He goes to bed in here, too," Mia pointed out. "He probably just wants to be around us."

"Now we know that Otis likes music, so he could be totally happy living with Pete," Michael said. He looked at Mom and Mia, hoping they would be as excited about this discovery as he was.

"Or maybe," Mia quickly added, "since Otis doesn't yowl in the night anymore, he could stay with us." She sat up straight and gave Mom a bright, shiny smile.

"Mia," Mom said gently. "That isn't really an option right now. You know that." Mia sighed and slumped.

Otis walked over to the table and curled himself around Michael's legs. "Think about how much Otis likes Pete," Michael reminded Mia. "He jumps up in his lap like he's known him forever. Right, Otis?"

Oh, the boy's talking to me! I could use some good petting. I'll get him to pet me.

Otis jumped into Michael's lap. Michael hadn't expected that. "Hey, Otis," he said, giving him a long stroke from head to tail. His fur felt soft and smooth.

"Well, you've done a good job with him," Mom said. "He does seem to be settling down. He'll be a sweet kitten for someone." Mom looked at Otis and smiled.

The kitten stood on Michael's lap, arching his back each time Michael stroked his fur, and kneading Michael's leg with his sharp little claws. "The question is, does Pete want Otis?" Mom said.

"I think he does," Michael said. "He really likes Otis, and Otis likes him. He just needs to give Otis another chance, and a little more time to settle in at his house."

"Well, it sounds like you're pretty sure. But Pete might need a little help figuring it out."

"I have an idea," Michael said. He jumped up, careful to keep hold of the tabby kitten. "Let's print out that picture you took of Otis and Pete, Mia. Get the camera. We don't have much time before school."

Mia met Michael in the office nook. When he handed Otis to her, the kitten tapped her chin with his paw, making Mia giggle.

Michael connected the camera to the computer. "We can give the picture to Pete after school." Michael downloaded the photo and clicked the print button.

Michael watched as the color photo slid onto the printer tray. In the picture, Otis's golden eyes were happy. Pete was smiling down at him. "What a great picture. When he sees this, and hears about Otis liking music, Pete will have to change his mind," Michael said.

"And if Otis stays with Pete, we could visit him. We could see him all the time." Mia snuggled Otis close to her chest and kissed his butterscotch-colored head.

Michael grabbed the photo, rushed out of the office nook, and ran smack into Dad.

"Sorry, buddy," Dad said.

"That's okay," Michael said. "It didn't hurt."

"No, I mean I'm sorry I didn't know you still wanted Pete to take Otis. Mom just told me, but it was a little too late. I just returned a call from

a woman who left us a message after she saw your flyer. I told her she could meet Otis this afternoon." Dad looked down at Michael.

Michael felt his heart drop. Mia walked up next to him with Otis in her arms.

"But Otis likes music. If Pete knew that, I'm sure he'd change his mind about keeping him," Michael said. "Look, we printed out this picture and everything." Michael handed it to Dad. "They belong together—anybody can see that."

Dad smiled down the picture. "It's a terrific photo, Michael. But I'm not so sure Pete's ready to change his mind. We really need to give this woman a chance. She sounded nice."

Michael sighed and trudged away. He didn't even bother to get the photo back from Dad.

"Grab your backpack and your lunch," Dad called. "We have to leave for school."

All morning at school, Michael stewed about it. How could this be happening? That afternoon, someone might take Otis away forever. Otis, who

belonged with Pete! He wanted to blame Dad, but he knew he couldn't.

"What's the big deal?" Jackson asked at lunch. "Maybe the person who called will be a good owner for Otis. That's what matters, right? Finding him a good home?"

"I guess you're right," Michael said. "But I really wanted Pete to adopt Otis."

"You guys will foster another kitten soon. Get Pete to take that one."

"It's not that easy," Michael said. He crunched on a pretzel stick and tried to think of a way to explain. "You know how it is when we're on the court together?"

Jackson nodded. "Sure. It's the best. We don't even have to say a word to each other. We just know what the other guy is going to do."

"Exactly. It just kind of works. We're a good team." Michael took another bite. "It's the same with Otis and Pete. They'd make a good team."

"That makes sense," Jackson said. "So, maybe

Pete will change his mind. Or maybe the other person will also be a good match for Otis. One way or another, your family will do what's right for Otis. It's like you guys are a team, too." He took a bite of his hummus sandwich.

"Yeah," Michael agreed. Then he realized that he hadn't talked to Dad about the woman who was coming over. Would Dad know what questions to ask her? Would he know how to figure out who would make the best owner for Otis? Michael and Mia knew Otis better than anyone. Dad might need their help. They couldn't let Otis down.

CHAPTER TEN

Michael rushed Mia out of her classroom as soon as school was over. "Dad said he was interviewing that woman at three o'clock," he said. "The one who wants to adopt Otis. We have to hurry home."

"Why?" Mia asked, pulling on her backpack.

"Dad might need our help," Michael said. "I found a whole list of questions on the Internet so we can tell if she's the right owner for Otis."

"What about guitar class?" asked Mia.

Michael shook his head. "Otis is more important than my guitar class. At least, he is today."

They ran out the front doors and raced down the sidewalk. As they neared home, Michael noticed a small brown dog tied to the iron fence in front of their building. It didn't look like any breed in particular, just a happy little mutt.

"Hey, boy," he said.

The dog let out a few big, friendly woofs. His tongue hung out and his tail whipped back and forth. "Whoa," Michael said as the dog jumped up on him. "I just need to get in the gate, fella." Michael let Mia slide through ahead of him.

"There's a dog tied to our fence," Michael heard Mia say once he was inside.

"He's mine," said an unfamiliar voice. Michael guessed it came from the woman who wanted to adopt Otis. "His name is Ruffy."

"That's a good name for him," Michael said as he came into the room. Ruffy's owner looked nice. She had blond hair pulled back in a ponytail and a friendly smile.

"Hey, guys," Dad said from his rocking chair. "You're home early."

"Michael wanted to help," Mia said.

"Yeah," Michael said. "I made a list of questions

so we can figure out if Otis would be a good kitten for you." He pulled a piece of paper out of his backpack, ready to start down the list. "Number one," he began.

But Dad interrupted him. "Let's not get ahead of ourselves." He held up his hands and turned to their guest. "Julie, these are my kids, Michael and Mia. They're pretty crazy about Otis."

"That's great," Julie said. "He's a lucky kitten." Her smile softened.

"Why do you want to adopt a kitten?" Michael went ahead and asked question number one.

Julie looked surprised. "Well," she began, "I wanted to get a friend for Ruffy. I thought it might help him calm down a little."

Michael pictured the dog. He was cute, but he was also hyper and loud. Michael had a feeling that Otis wouldn't be too crazy about living with Ruffy. He took a deep breath, trying to figure out how to say so without hurting Julie's feelings.

"It's okay, Michael," Dad said. "It didn't take

us long to realize that Julie and Ruffy wouldn't be the best family for Otis."

"Ruffy scared Otis when he came in," Julie said. "Otis ran to the back of the house." She motioned to Michael's room. "That's why I tied Ruffy outside."

"Julie and I were just saying good-bye," Dad explained.

"Oh," Michael said. "Okay, then. Well, it was nice meeting you." He gave Julie a quick wave and hurried to his room to find Otis. Mia followed him.

"Otis?" Michael called. "You all right, buddy?" Michael got down on his knees and looked under the bed. Sure enough, Otis was huddled up in the far corner. He looked back at Michael with wide, frightened eyes.

It's the boy and girl. I'm glad to see them, but I'm staying put. I'll stay right here until I know for sure that dog is gone.

"How are we going to get him out?" Mia asked.

"I guess we'll just give him time," Michael said. "We don't want to reach in for him. He wouldn't like that."

They waited for a few minutes, but Otis didn't come out. Michael put some music on the iPod, but the kitten stayed under the bed. Finally, Mia got bored and left, and a little while later Otis came tiptoeing out. Michael scooped him up onto his lap and petted him under his chin, smiling when he felt the familiar tickle of the kitten's purr.

When Otis fell asleep, Michael laid him onto the shirt by the speakers. Then he got out his guitar to practice a little. Guitar class must be almost over by now, and in a way he was sorry he had skipped it. If only he'd had the chance to show that picture to Pete. He strummed softly and Otis barely stirred in his sleep.

A little later, Dad called down the hallway. "You guys want a snack?" Before Michael or Mia could respond, the doorbell rang. "Oh, that must be the other person who called about adopting Otis. I'll get it."

"What? Dad!" Michael called.

"If Julie's not taking him, we want Pete to have him!" Mia yelled. Michael heard her run out of her room and pound down the hall after Dad.

Michael flopped down on his bed, too mad to even go see who the other person was. He couldn't believe that Dad would let someone else see Otis. How could he?

A few moments later, Michael heard footsteps heading toward his room. Otis must have heard them, too, because he woke up and dashed back under the bed. "Stay under there, Otis," Michael whispered. "If they can't find you, they can't take you away." Then he heard a familiar voice.

"Where is the little dude?"

"I think he's in Michael's room," said Dad. "Hey, Michael. Pete's here."

Pete appeared in the doorway. Mia ducked her head under his elbow, and Dad stood just behind them. As always, Pete had his guitar slung over his shoulder.

Michael sat up. "What are you doing here?"

"Your dad gave me a great photo this morning." Pete pulled the picture out of his back pocket and looked at it. "Thanks for printing it out."

"I helped," Mia said. She looked up at Pete and smiled.

"Yeah, Mia helped," Michael said. He fiddled with the seam on his pillow. Pete still hadn't explained why he was there.

"I guess seeing this picture made me miss Otis," Pete said. "I came over as soon as I was done with guitar class."

"Otis missed you, too," Michael said. He sat up straighter. He had all kinds of things to tell Pete, and now was the time to do it. "You know, Otis doesn't like to sleep when it's too quiet, so I played my iPod for him and he slept in my room

all night. I bet he really liked your guitar playing. He was just scared of the drums."

Pete nodded, smiling. "I had a feeling it might be the drums," he said. "I was thinking I could ask one of my friends if he would host band practice for a while. That would give Otis more time to feel at home. I don't think I gave us enough of a chance. With a little time, I think we could be really good together."

"You mean . . . you're going to adopt him?" Michael asked.

Pete grinned. "I was thinking I might. And now that you're telling me he does like music after all, I definitely want to—if I pass the Battelli test, that is," he said.

"We'd all be happy if you adopted Otis," Dad said.

"Dad's right. But first you'll have to get him out from under the bed," Mia said. She bent down and peeked at the kitten.

Pete sat down on the floor. "Let's test Michael's theory. We'll see if he really likes music." Pete unzipped his case and pulled out his guitar. "Hey, Otis," he said. "Will you come on out and play?" Pete strummed a few chords and hummed along.

Michael peered under the bed to look at Otis. The kitten's whiskers twitched and his eyes were shining.

Oh, that guy with the low voice is back. Maybe he scared the dog away. I like the sounds he's making. I'll see if the coast is clear.

"There he is!" Pete practically sang the words as Otis crept out from under the bed. The kitten looked around and sniffed the air. He kneaded the carpet with his paws. Then he walked over to Pete, climbed into his lap, and began to purr in time to the music.

I had a feeling this guy would come back. I had a really good feeling.

Pete put down the guitar and picked up Otis. "Hey, little dude," he said as he touched his nose to Otis's. "I think we could have lots of fun together. Want to come home with me?"

"What's all the excitement?" Mom said, poking her head in the door. "Hey, Pete."

"Mom! Mom! Pete is going to adopt Otis!" Mia said.

"Well, I'm glad to hear it," Mom said. She looked at Michael with a knowing smile.

Michael watched as Mia dangled a string just out of Otis's reach. The kitten leapt for it. Otis looked proud when he caught it in his mouth.

Michael smiled. Jackson was right. His family really was a team. If Mom hadn't had the idea to put up posters, if Mia hadn't taken the great picture of Pete and Otis together, if Dad hadn't given it to Pete, and if Michael hadn't told Pete that Otis really did like music, then Otis might still be looking for a home. But they had all worked together, and look what had happened! Michael couldn't wait to find out what kind of kitty his team would foster next.

KITTY CORNER CAT QUIZ

When Michael talked to Dr. Bulford, the vet at Wags and Whiskers, she told him about some ways to help Otis feel at home. What do you think might help a kitty get used to a new place?

A. Try to hold the cat as much as possible.

B. Give the cat time and space to get used to your home.

C. Chase the cat from room to room.

D. Invite all your friends to meet the cat at once.

Turn the page for the answer.

The answer is B. Cats are very independent, and they like to figure things out for themselves. A cat may need a few hours — or a few months — to get used to a new home. It's important to give the cat time to explore the house and become comfortable there. For the first few days, you may even want to keep your cat in one room so he can get used to your home little by little.

Soon your cat will begin to explore. After all, cats are curious! Your kitty will want to check out every nook and cranny. Make sure that the cat has a special place where no one will bother him. Cats often feel safe in small spaces. Remember how Otis liked to disappear under tables and beds? Allow your kitty to hide if he is scared. Don't force him to come out. Make sure your cat knows he can trust you.

Of course, you'll want your friends to meet your cat. Take it nice and slow. Invite one friend over at a time. Let your kitty choose how close he wants to get and if he wants to be petted.

If you've taken in a stray or adopted a shelter cat, you probably don't know a lot about what kind of life the cat had before he met you. Some cats will let you know what they like or don't like right away, while other cats are more private and shy. Taking the time to get to know your new kitty will help him feel more at home. Plus it's fun to learn about all the funny quirks that make your cat . . . *your* cat.

WHERE EVERY PUPPY FINDS A HOME

■SCHOLASTIC

www.scholastic.com

www.ellenmiles.net

Read them all!

PUPPLSP11

ABOUT THE AUTHOR

ELLEN MILES loves dogs, which is why she has a great time writing The Puppy Place books. And guess what? She loves cats, too! (In fact, her very first pet was a beautiful tortoiseshell cat named Jenny.) That's why she came up with a brand-new series called Kitty Corner. Ellen lives in Vermont and loves to be outdoors every day, walking, biking, skiing, or swimming, depending on the season. She also loves to read, cook, explore her beautiful state, play with dogs, and hang out with friends and family.

Visit Ellen at **www.ellenmiles.net**.